W9-BRQ-950

Joe Moves In
A First-Week Scrapbook

by Adam Scott
illustrated by David B. Levy

Property of
Bradley Beach Public Library

Simon Spotlight/Nick Jr.
New York   London   Toronto   Sydney   Singapore

To Angela for creating such a welcoming house for Joe to move into—A. S.
For a very special cat, Chimney—D. B. L.

Note to Parents from Creators:
Blue's new friend Joe just moved in! He made this special scrapbook to help him remember his first week with all of his new friends. Your child will learn all about Steve's brother, Joe—and his duck, Boris—while exploring ways of adapting comfortably to new situations and making friends feel welcome in a new environment.

Based on the TV series *Blue's Clues*® created by Traci Paige Johnson,
Todd Kessler, and Angela C. Santomero as seen on Nick Jr.®
On *Blue's Clues*, Joe is played by Donovan Patton. Photos by Joan Marcus.

SIMON SPOTLIGHT
An imprint of Simon & Schuster Children's Publishing Division
1230 Avenue of the Americas, New York, New York 10020
Copyright © 2002 Viacom International Inc.
All rights reserved. NICKELODEON, NICK JR., *Blue's Clues*, and all related titles, logos,
and characters are trademarks of Viacom International Inc.
All rights reserved, including the right of reproduction in whole or in part in any form.
SIMON SPOTLIGHT and colophon are registered trademarks of Simon & Schuster.
Manufactured in the United States of America
First Edition   10 9 8 7 6 5 4 3
ISBN 0-689-84943-5

Hi, it's me, Joe! This is my scrapbook. I made it to help me remember my first week in my new home with my new friends. Take a look!

I brought my camera so I can take lots of pictures. Here's a picture of my brother, Steve. I took it just before he went away to college. I'm going to miss him, but we'll send letters to each other.

I won't miss my duck, Boris, because he's going to live here too. Boris likes having his picture taken.

Tickety Tock wakes me up bright and early every morning. One morning I woke up extra early and took Tickety's picture. . . . She sure was surprised!

Blue wakes up early too, but Boris likes to sleep late.

Oops! I forgot to bring my toothbrush. But guess who gave me a brand-new toothbrush with blue squares all over it? That's right! Slippery Soap. I just had to take a picture.

Boris already made three new friends!

Oh—guess what else I brought from my old home to my new home. . . . My favorite clothes! Here's a picture of my favorite shirts in my favorite colors.

Orange

Blue

Purple

Yellow

Red

Green

I love them all. Which is your favorite?

One morning Mr. Salt and Mrs. Pepper made strawberry pancakes for breakfast. Yum! Here is the picture Mrs. Pepper took of me at the table.

Look at the family pictures I took. Everyone's saying "cheese!"

Clue 1

Clue 2

Clue 3

We played Blue's Clues, but I didn't have a
notebook. So I took pictures of the clues instead.
And do you know what? I figured out Blue's Clues
all by myself!

The answer was Sidetable Drawer. Can you guess what was in Sidetable's drawer? It was my very own handy-dandy notebook that Blue made for me!

I had the best time playing hide-and-seek with Shovel and Pail. So did Boris. I found the greatest hiding place—but Pail found me anyway and took a picture. Oh, well.

I guess Boris found a better hiding place than I did. Can you find him?

I met my neighbor, Periwinkle. He did a great
magic trick with his cape where he made Boris
disappear. At first I was a little scared, but then Boris
appeared again.

Periwinkle collects things that roll. I took pictures of some of his collection.

Look! This is a picture of my first letter. Mailbox brought it to me. It was from all my new friends!

I had no idea what their special surprise was. Do you?

Go to the
Kitchen
for a special
surprise!

Property of
Bradley Beach Public Library

★ Welcome, Joe! ★

The special surprise was a party—just for me! This is a picture of everyone shouting, "Welcome, Joe!" Everybody shouted for Boris, too. I know I'm going to love it here. So will Boris.

What a great first week in my new house! I wonder what we'll do tomorrow.

My First Week